Alligators Ain't All

A body by the canal. "Old Rocky" is blamed – but there ain't no way that alligator did that.

Contents

About the author

CD Moulton has traveled extensively over much of the world both in the music business, where he was a rock guitarist, songwriter and arranger and in an import/export business. He has been everything from a bar owner to auto salvage (junkyard) manager, longshoreman to high steel worker, orchid grower to landscaper, tropical fish farmer to commercial fisherman. He started writing books in 1983 and has published more than 250 books as of January 1, 2015. His most popular books to date are about research with orchids, though much of his science fiction and fantasy work has proven popular. He wrote the CD Grimes, PI series and the Det. Nick Storie series, Clint Faraday series and many other works.

He now resides in Gualaca, Chiriqui, Panamá, where he writes books, plays music with friends, does research with orchids and medicinal plants – and pursues his favorite ways to spend his time: beach bum and roaming the mountain jungles doing his botanical research. He has lately become involved in fighting for the rights of the indigenous people, who are among his closest friends, and in fighting the extreme corruption in the courts and police in Panamá.

He offers the free e-book, *Fading Paradise*, that explains what he has been through because of the corruption.

CD is the discoverer of the Chadam Protocol for curing cancer. Facebook page Ambrosia peruviana for cancer

The Body

Al Rhamer took his coffee outside to stand on the dock to watch the sunrise. He liked the quiet in the morning and he liked to watch "Old Rocky" cruising around the canal.

Old Rocky was a twelve foot alligator that came and went. He had been around for about a week and would leave again in a couple of days. He'd be back in maybe a month or so.

Landon Forbes was going out in his boat. He went out every Tuesday and Saturday.

What the hell kind of name was Landon? Cripes.

Nice enough guy, though, if a little snobby. Wife was a pill, most of the time. Knew she wanted a favor if she was suddenly nice.

Oh, well. You get used to the people who live close around you. Except for Sam Levant. Nobody knew anything about him. A real nut-case. Would it break his neck to at least nod at neighbors? Landon had seemed very friendly with him the first time Al saw them together in the vacant lot next door, sharing some kind of joke. Al had stepped around the eleagnus right beside them almost where they had been chatting. They must have been talking about someone, though Landon wasn't that type, and thought he overheard them. They both seemed just a bit embarrassed and nervous. Landon had chilled toward Sam suddenly, after that.

Maybe because Gladys was a bit too friendly with him. She might have ... well, it was none of his business. He might be reading more into it than was there. He didn't like Levant and he didn't, to be totally honest about it, like Gladys.

Lucy Goodall waved, he waved back. She threw the leftover breakfast Todd didn't finish in the canal to watch the catfish eat it.

Too many catfish in the canal, but that's what happens when they build all those highrises upstream. Pollutes the whole damned canal. Nothing you can do about it because the commissioners are owned body and soul by the developers.

Old Rocky went to the far bank and tried to climb out, but it was too steep ... was that somebody laying in those blackberries over there? Somebody in white pants and a red shirt?

Old Rocky wouldn't try to get up there to him. He had learned to stay away from people over the years, being thumped on the head with oars and poles if he got too close.

"Hey! Hey you! Over there!" Al yelled, but the guy didn't move. Landon was getting in his boat, so called to ask what was going on. The guy was over on his side of the canal, so he couldn't see him. Al yelled that there was somebody over there and Old Rocky was trying to get to him.

"Oh, shit!" Landon cried. "Rock wouldn't go after anybody who moved! Is he asleep ... I guess not, or he'd wake up when you yelled. I'll check it out. Maybe he's hurt or sick or something."

Landon started his motor and went to look at the guy laying there. "Oh, Jesus! His whole throat's ripped out! Jesus Christ! Call nine one one, Al. There ain't no way that one's alive! Looks like Old Rock already got to him!"

Todd came to his dock to ask what was going on and Landon called that there was a dead body over there. Some old guy.

"Ain't from around here, I don't think," Todd said, then turned to yell at the house, "Hey! Luce! Call nine one one! Landon found a body!"

"Not *me*!" Landon shot back. "*Al* found him!"

"Rocky! Not me!" Al answered.

Landon grinned and flipped him a finger.

"It looks to me like a gator got him," Lt. Michael Kersey announced, after spending about five minutes looking around the scene. "Dumb-asses will fool with them. Don't have sense enough to know their brain's the size of a walnut.

"You agree, Millie?"

Dr. Millie Dorman, the CSI team head, grunted, took another look around the area, walked close to the water's edge and across to where Old Rocky was sitting next to Al Rhamer's dock. Rhamer and the snooty neighbor, Gladys Forbes, were standing on the dock, watching them. Lucy Goodall and her husband, Todd, were in a boat with Landon Forbes, who she had met. He worked for a medical supply company.

"I've got some questions," Millie said, grimacing. "Like, how did he get up here? Lividity says he didn't die here. Could be close, but not this spot."

"Rolled over in the water when he got drug up here," Sgt. Norton said. "Mike has it tagged. The idiot's brain isn't any bigger than the 'gator's. This is the result of some stupid tourist trying to feed a 'gator, I'd say.

"That how you see it, Mike?"

Millie grunted again, but looked puzzled. "No drag marks."

"It's wire grass, mostly," Kersey replied. "It won't show us much. Dry as it is, there wouldn't be marks if you drove a Sherman Tank across it.

"You got a TOD?"

"Tentatively, I'd give it as six to seven hours. Put it at two to three AM. I'll get it a lot closer at the lab.

"Okay. You got the pictures done, Art?"

Art Pelt, her assistant, gave her the high sign and she went to turn the body over. "No ID," she said, after going through his pockets. "Hmm. Drives a Lexus. No watch, nothing much else. A few cents in pocket change. Pants unzipped. Car and door keys, no others.

"Art, get some pictures of this. It could be from dragging, but it doesn't quite fit."

"What?" Kersey asked.

"Blood pooled there," Millie said, ignoring Kersey. "Looks like some transfer here. Get a close-up and I'll mark it for the DNA lab.

"Hmm-mm. Two teeth broken, but there's no penetration marks. Big bruise on the lips. I'd say fifteen to twenty minutes before death.

"No shoes?

"Defensive wounds to the hands. Could be teeth scrapes, but aren't consistent with the size teeth of a gator big enough to do the rest of it. I'll bag those hands.

"Okay. That's pretty much what I can find on the body. Let me do a quick review of the scene and we can transport.

"Art, you've got pictures?"

"Yeah!"Art answered. "Every inch, still and video."

"Okay. Give me some good closeups of the wounds from several angles. I don't know if those teeth marks are ... right."

Art nodded and took some more pictures.

She spent about ten minutes more checking around from very close and had Art take a couple of pictures, one of a small penknife/keychain with two keys on it about three feet from the body. One was a Master padlock key and the other a Schlage house key.

"Okay. Transport team!" she ordered. Two attendants brought a Gurney over to bag and load the body. A few minutes later Millie and Art climbed into the lab wagon and left. Lt. Kersey called that he'd drive over to Al's place to get their reports.

"Okay. You got to your dock about five minutes before Mr. Forbes called nine one one?" Kersey asked AL, looking at his watch and tapping the Bic pen on the clipboard impatiently. "You then stayed right here on the dock. You didn't see or hear anything last night or in the wee hours. That about it?"

"Lucy called you, but that's about it."

"You were fixing to go out in the gulf in your boat," he continued, turning to face Landon. "Mr. Kramer called that someone was hurt or sick and you went to check and found him, then Kramer called to Todd, who told his wife to call nine one one?"

"Who the Sam hell is Kramer?" Landon demanded. "That about covers it, except Mr. *Rhamer* called to me."

"Whatever," Kersey replied, scribbling on his pad. Norton let a little smirk show for a second.

"Patrolman Corby, I made the call when Todd called to me, then you and Patrolman Merton showed up about fifteen minutes later, along with that Dr. Dorman," Lucy said innocently. "Nobody heard or saw anything last night or in the wee hours this morning. It's a very quiet neighborhood, usually.

"Old Rocky didn't kill the guy. A 'gator will drag its prey into the water, not take it out."

Kersey colored, Norton snickered, then Kersey said, "Point made and taken. We do that to get a reaction."

"So do I," Lucy said. Kersey laughed and said he liked her. No crap.

"Well, except that I think the 'gator killed him, I should have it all," Kersey said. "If there's anything else we need we have ways to contact you."

"What's going on here? What's all the excitement? Cops in *this* neighborhood?" Sam Levant said, coming from the lot next door. "I just got home. What did I miss?"

"Al found a body," Gladys Forbes said. (She was the only one in the group who got along with Levant). "It seems that disgusting reptile killed a tourist."

"Which disgusting reptile?" Levant asked. "The Dorner jerk?"

"Rocky didn't kill him," Landon said, giving Gladys a hard look. "There's no way he could even get up on that bank, much less drag a hundred eighty pound body up there!"

"Uh-huh," Al agreed. "Not to mention, he was dry."

Kersey looked shocked and Norton let out a little explosive snort. "How could you tell that?" Kersey asked. "You said you didn't go over there."

"That red shirt wouldn't be that bright if it was wet," Al pointed out. "Red turns dark when it's wet."

"And it leaves a strong stain anywhere it's dragged, so he wasn't dragged there with a wet red shirt," Lucy said. "Those white pants would have pink streaks all over them. They were so white they glared. Those pants would have been almost transparent if they were wet."

Kersey shrugged and said they had some further investigating to do, but nothing was inconsistent with a 'gator attack.

"The pants were unzipped, so he probably was going to take a quick leak in the canal and the 'gator happened to be right there," Norton suggested. Kersey gave him a look and said they'd better head in. They'd wait for the forensics reports to tell them where to go next.

"To Dunkin Donuts, I'd guess," Lucy said. "He's got this one figured and a videotape of something else happening wouldn't change his mind.

"Did you catch that, Al?"

"Catch what?" Levant asked.

"Yeah. Norton wasn't supposed to tell us his pants were unzipped," Landon said. "I caught that."

"What the hell difference would that make to a dead guy?" Levant asked.

"I don't have a clue," Al answered. "I do know there are a lot of reasons to unzip your pants that don't have anything to do with taking a leak in a canal."

"Yeah. I guess so. Three in the morning, probably for a hooker," Levant said. "Who was he?"

"They don't know yet, except he drives a Lexus," Gladys said. "That obnoxious Sgt. Norton kept asking about us seeing a Lexus around.

"I mean, in *this* neighborhood? *Half* of us have Lexuses!"

"Maybe somebody saw something that means his killer drives a Lexus," Todd said.

"I thought Rocky was supposed to have killed him?" Levant asked.

"There's too much 'was supposed to' in this," Al replied, thinking. "More and more doesn't quite fit. I think all hell's going to break loose on this one!"

"Hi, Nort," Kersey greeted. "Learning anything about the alligator case?"

"Well, Millie says she can't rule anything in or out. She says she doesn't think there's a chance it was really an alligator attack. Too many little things that don't fit. She could probably prove it in court, but she would have to get a lot of stuff she's not going to get.

"Any idea who he is ... was?"

"There's a Lexus out by forty one that's been there since the night before. I'm taking the keys he was carrying out to see if they fit. If so, he was Daniel P. Gorse, from Lubbock, Texas. Moved here in ninety eight.

"Want to ride along? I'll drive the Lexus in if it's his."

"Won't Millie want to look it over first?"

"Nah. Waste of time. She'll check it out when she has time at the lot," Kersey said, stretching. Norton got up and they went in a cruiser to the Lexus. The keys fit, so Kersey drove it to the impound lot while Norton followed in the cruiser. They went over the car, but there wasn't much there.

"Could he have gotten to that canal from where he left the car?" Norton asked when they were back in the station.

"Way I see it, he met a hooker and they went out there in her car," Kersey replied, pouring a cup of the awful office coffee for himself. "She rolled him and took off, then the gator found him there and took a bite."

"A gator would drag him into the water. They never take stuff out of the water. We both know that!"

"Uh-uh. Not if something scared him off. Way I see it, lights from a car going around the corner across that vacant lot next to Rhamer's flashed on him and he would dive. Fast."

"What about those two missing teeth?"

"The hooker smacked him with something, knocked his

teeth out when it knocked him out, she took off."

"That would explain a lot of it. It has a certain logic. I guess the other things will fall into place. We just have to find them."

"If we look for them hard enough, we'll find them. I'd rather write it up as what we know it is, but those people out there are the type who'll cause all kinds of grief if we don't make a show of some kind."

"I was really sort of surprised about those people. I mean, those snobby types of places don't usually have that kind of mix. Rhamer's black, Levant's a Jew, Forbes and Goodall and the Mrs. Forbes are all your standard whites. Gladys Forbes has a lot of Oriental blood. I saw Rhamer's wife for a minute or so. She's India Indian, I'd say. Maybe an Arab mix."

"What's up? You want to get accused of racial profiling, now?" Kersey asked. Norton grinned and flipped him a finger. His wife was Hispanic. He wasn't close to being a bigot, but Kersey tended to be a bit of one. If the body had been black and the onlookers white, they would as much as drop it right there and then

They finished their coffee and donuts, then took the cruiser out to the scene. They spent over an hour carefully looking over the area and Kersey found where a car had pulled in off the road under an oak tree. They took pictures, then went to study along the bank. There were some rocks piled in the water and up the bank about fifty feet down the canal that Kersey said a gator could have climbed. There was a little clod knocked off the bank directly below where the body was found that Kersey said was probably made when the gator dove off of it. Norton didn't point out that it was where Forbes' boat had hit the bank. Why bother? Kersey had decided it happened the way he described it. The report was going to support that. Period.

Norton didn't care. Don't make waves. That's a good way

to find yourself back doing road patrol. It was nothing to him. The boss isn't always right, but he's always the boss.

"I guess we really should make a cast of the tire tracks here," Norton suggested. "That Gladys woman and the Levant asshole are standing over there watching us.

"You noticed how none of them except the Gladys woman seemed to want to have anything to do with him?"

"He said something that made the other men back away from him. I missed what it was. Maybe it's something personal. Guy comes on to the wives or something."

"I don't see any wives wanting anything to do with him. He's a Dr. Fell."

"A what? Some kind of local expression?" Kersey asked, pouring the P of P onto the tracks.

"An old rhyme. Burns or somebody, I think. I do not like thee, Dr. Fell. The reason why I cannot tell. But this I know, and know it well. I do not like thee, Dr. Fell."

"Hmm. It fits that one. Ten minutes to set. Looks like a standard sort of tread to me. Sort of narrow, but not very distinctive."

"Yeah. Offset odd angles, so it will be Michellin, but I can't say which one. High end, by the breaks. Probably the hooker drives a foreign sports job. Means she's expensive, but he had a Lexus, so he could afford her."

"Yeah. Let's go over there and ask if there's been a fancy foreign sports job around that they noticed. Make them think we're onto something."

They waited until the cast was set, marked it, took some pictures and loaded it into the trunk of the cruiser, then went to talk to the two standing in the lot next to Rhamer's.

"The only sports cars I've seen here are Sam's and Bill Awkrights, down on Penter Circle," Gladys said. "Sam doesn't come to our side of the canal much and Bill never. It's a dead end right there where you were parked, so there's no reason they would.

"Did you find anything new?"

"His name was Gorse, he's from Texas a couple of years back and he probably came out here with a hooker, sorry ma'am, in a sports car," Kersey answered, acting like he was reading something on his clipboard. "She rolled him and left him laying there, unconscious, and a gator tried to drag him to the water, but got scared off."

"Yeah. Hookers do bring tricks out there sometimes," Levant said.

"They do? I didn't know that!" Gladys cried.

"Late. We can see them parked over there and you can't see cars there from your side. Houses in the way. Not a lot, but sometimes."

"You didn't happen to see one that night?" Norton asked.

"Well, I got home about two thirty or three. Was bar-hopping ... but not drunk! I only had a beer in four bars over five hours ... to listen to the bands. I didn't look. I may have seen like a dash or dome light glow, sort of, but I can't say if it was then or some other night, you know? I see them so much I don't pay any attention. That is, not unless it's a really bright one, and that means there was nothing really bright last night, I guess. I can't ... I'd have to say not."

"Cars go by with those loud boom box things sometimes late at night, but they get reported if they stop or come back more than once," Gladys volunteered. "I never have understood how anyone can be in the same car with one of those things!"

"Makes the whole neighborhood sound like down in ni ... uh, I mean, in one of those slum ghetto places," Levant complained. "Like those wetback camps. Loud and vulgar. That rap excuse for music they play all the time in nig ... in the, you know, slum places."

Norton bit back his retort. He glanced at Kersey, who had a sneer on his face. It was becoming more than clear why nobody in the neighborhood liked Sam Levant.

"It just does not *fit* in this place!" Gladys agreed. "I mean, we're a lot more, what they call diverse, than most of the better areas ... than most places, if you know what I mean. We could use a tiny bit more respect for the proprieties of society, if you ask me!"

Or why she and Levant got along.

"Nobody did," Kersey said, shortly. "We were asking about last night.

"So nobody saw or heard anything. We have a little evidence to process. It can get pretty much muddled in these neighborhoods where hookers hang out. There's so much that hasn't got anything to do with this case. If you've got hookers, you've got druggies and pimps and dealers and all that"

"Whatever in the *world*!" Gladys cried. "Hookers do *not* hang out here! I have never ... that's slanderous! I'm going to lodge a complaint against you for that! There are no *drug dealers* around here! The idea! I'm going to file a complaint!"

"Give it a go," Norton shot back. "Captain Kiley is in charge of internal affairs, so you can go to him, direct. Before you do, you might want to take note that there's a tape recorder sitting right there in plain view, a videocam on the dash of the cruiser. Mr. Levant said, very clearly, that hookers park over there so often that he wouldn't notice or remember which night any particular one was there. That sure sounds like hookers hang out here to me! You said, yourself, that they play loud boom boxes late at night."

"What..!? I didn't say...! I mean, that's not what I meant!" Levant protested.

"We can't go by what you meant, only by what you said," Kersey replied, reasonably. "After all, we're not mind readers.

"Well, Nort. Let's take this stuff in and process it."

They headed back to the station. They got the giggles over how they got back at those two snobs.

"Why is it the ones who might have a reason to be snobs never are, but cruds like those two always are?" Norton wondered. "I wish I wasn't a cop, sometimes. I'd kick that obnoxious prick's ass and smack that stinking broad in the mouth so fast they wouldn't know what hit them!"

"No, you wouldn't. I feel the same way about them, but it's not in our nature ... well, mine, maybe a little, but not yours. You'd never hit a woman ... in that way. You sure as hell smacked them both in the chops with the report bit! I think she would rather have been smacked physically! After all! Think what it would mean to the *station* of the area if the police told the newspapers *hookers* and *drug dealers* hung around! What would the better class people *think*?

"That Levant character ... you know, I think those two are probably having a little affair. His answers keep getting tangled up in themselves. Here they are in the middle of the afternoon, when hubby's at work, hanging around on his side of the canal. I wish there was some way to let Forbes know about it. Maybe he'd smack them both around for us! We could report it as self defense with Levant and accidental injury for her!"

Norton giggled again.

"We have a lot more to go on now than a few hours ago," Millie reported, pouring herself a cup of the awful office coffee. "No gator did that, but we aren't going to be able to sit in front of a jury and say it's proven. There will be doubt, if only because a defense lawyer plants it. The only thing different from what you say is that the hooker or the hooker and her pimp killed him and set it up.

"I saw the tape of your run-in with those two prime examples of prime examples. The whole station is getting a kick out of how you put them in their place. You have to see those two are spending their afternoons in beddy-bye while the husband paying her bills is working his ass off to support her.

"I'd say she was the type to turn tricks under the spreading oaks down the street, but she wouldn't have the guts to kill anyone, much less in such a messy way.

"Maybe you can just tag this case as an unresolved, but probably a death by alligator or something.

"God! This coffee is vile! Doesn't anyone ever clean that urn?"

"It tastes even worse when we do," Kersey said. "We already put the case in the pending case drawer. We can't waste our time looking for something we know we don't have a snowflake's chance of solving before we start."

Millie sighed, said that was the trouble with police work anymore. Too many of them were things that they would never solve.

She went back to her office, and Kersey and Norton headed out to a suspicious death in a nursing home.

<u>*Al Rhamer Looks Around*</u>

Al Rhamer watched Gladys Forbes drive away from Sam Levant's place as he turned into his drive.

What was she doing there?

Well, she wasn't any of his business. He didn't much care for her and he most certainly didn't like Levant and didn't care who knew it.

He was glad his wife, Tarisha, (he called her "Trish" most of the time. The neighbors had picked that up) didn't socialize with either of those two. He wished she had more friends, but her cultural background meant that she wouldn't. She seemed perfectly content and was certainly everything any man could want in a wife.

Lucy waved to him when he went down to the dock to see what, if anything, was changed across the canal. There was a yellow crime scene tape, but that was all he could see. It looked normal to him. Old Rocky slipped out of the mangroves beside the dock and sat floating about fifty feet away, watching him.

"Rock, you resent the implications, don't you?" Al asked. "You didn't have a thing to do with that dead guy over there.

"Old Rock, there's a lot about that mess that isn't quite right."

Lucy called across that the cops had come back and had talked to (stressed) Gladys and Sam in the lot next to his house for over an hour. Call her.

He promised that he'd call her in a few minutes. She waved again. She would have pumped Gladys for everything the cops found. Lucy sounded almost like she was having fun when she said to call her, so maybe it was something juicy. He wondered if maybe it was more about Gladys and Sam than what the cops found.

Maybe the cops found something juicy about Gladys and

Sam? That would be a hoot!

Al went inside and spent a few minutes with Trish that contained a lot of touching and giggling. They always had fun when there was no one around to be outraged by their playing.

Al called Lucy. It seemed the cops found the dead guy's ("victim's" according to that Kersey ass) name. Gorse, from Texas. A hooker had killed him, then Old Rocky had tried to drag him into the water, or something. She told him about the meeting and was having a lot of fun with the cops telling the snooty Gladys that a bunch of hookers and drug dealers were hanging around the neighborhood.

They talked for awhile, then Al hung up.

He couldn't swallow that. Not for one minute. Rock didn't "try" to drag him into the water. He'd *be* in the water if that had happened. Something was very fishy, and it wasn't an odor from the canal. Someone was trying to cover this up, if you asked him. Some people knew a lot more than they were letting on while others were trying to steer this so-called investigation.

Well, Al Rhamer worked with comps for hours a day and he knew how to find things on them. He was sure there was something to be found here. About those cops and about the "victim" and hookers. Maybe there was also something about people in the neighborhood. Al had never gone to the comps to check on anyone in the area, but there had never before been any reason for him to do so.

Okay. You can Google anybody. Al had once put his own name on the engine and there had been four items about him and computer science that he never knew existed before that moment. He also knew there was no other Allen Rhamer on the site.

The victim's name, according to Lucy, was Daniel Gorse. Originally from somewhere in Texas. Al typed that in and noted several people by that name. One of them had owned a clothiers in Lubbock, Texas, until 1997. That would be the one he wanted.

Born April 28, 1936, Littletown, Texas.

Schooling through high school in East Littletown.

Attended Texas International Business Institution two years and got a degree in business administration. Average grades.

Worked as a general construction laborer for two years, then as a head bartender in a booze joint for three years in Lubbock. The Bouncy Butterfly.

If that wasn't a gay joint he never heard of one!

Nothing except for two arrests for excessive speed in Louisiana in 1987 and again in 1988 and an affray in Houston in 1988. Charges were subsequently dropped on the affray by mutual consent.

Affray? Mutual consent? Affray was more than a couple of thugs duking it out. How many were involved in that one?

He opened the file on the arrest number. Eight men fighting at a bar called Double Dealers.

A check on the Double Dealers showed it was a swingers' bar that catered to bisexuals. Basis seemed to be that some of the wives didn't much appreciate the husbands making it together, then someone insulted the wives, then it got out of hand. Somebody had AIDS or was suspected of having AIDS or some such thing.

Al was glad he'd never played those kinds of idiot games.

Back to the resume.

Opened a clothiers in Lubbock in 1988.

Next heard of when he ended up dead of undetermined cause under suspicious circumstances, in Lee County, Florida.

Very little there, really. Lubbock, he might have been where he knew about illegal aliens or drug routes and distributors.

Wait a minute. When were those speeding tickets?

Hmm. Returning home from Mardi Gras. Bartender in a gay bar. Affray in a bisexual bar. He definitely wasn't out here with some hooker. Maybe with a trick, but he would have been in his own car, if that were the case.

Well, maybe he was the trick, but he wasn't married, so wouldn't be looking for sex in a car somewhere at his age. He'd be in bed in his nice luxurious apartment or at a motel, where he could be comfortable.

Did he have a luxurious apartment?

Al went to the phone book, then to the unlisted section with his code from work. Dan Gorse had the penthouse at Royal Golden Sunset Condos. He would definitely not have been having paid sex in a car, particularly a cramped sports car. D. Gorse also had one hell of a lot more money than he made in any clothiers, even as the owner.

Well, that was something to go on.

Nothing there about the cops, Kersey and Norton, or the CSI woman, Mildred Dorman. Very typical.

Gladys Forbes, nee Gladys Spinet-Moseley. Atlanta, Georgia, 1968. Rather little. All the best schools and nothing out of line. One ticket in 1995 for running a red light. That was a letdown. Al wanted something on her.

Samuel Levant, Tahoes, New Mexico, 1965. Nothing except for writing a book about flying saucers in 1988 that sold a total of about 300 copies. Vanity publisher. Had a collaboration try with a Markus Garner about desert insects that didn't do even that well.

Landon Forbes, Todd and Lucy Goodall, nothing.

Might as well check on Markus Garner.

Not much. Worked for a newspaper chain, Phoenix Branch, then moved to Orlando in 2004 to run the editorial offices of the chain there.

There wasn't any connection with any of them.

Was there? Damn it! Something was far from right about this whole stupid mess!

Al had a lot of books about UFO's. He'd studied a lot about them and had come to the conclusion there wasn't any solid evidence for their existence, but also nothing convincing against them. He tended to agree with that letter in the Bonita Banner that said the reason no alien intelligence had contacted us was because they are intelligent.

He looked at the titles of the UFO books on the shelf and pulled out a couple editions. He didn't have Levant's book, but almost no one did have it – or want it.

The list of articles on the cover of one of the books immediately caught his eye. "The Lubbock Lights" was about strange lights seen by everyone from the sheriff to the local banker in Lubbock over a period of several nights.

Well, there was a possible connection! Levant might have gone to Lubbock to research his book. Had he gone to a gay bar and met one Daniel Gorse? Maybe a bisexual swingers' bar?

Al went back to re-read the arrest records, but the names given were "unconfirmed" for the most part.

Which didn't mean Levant *wasn't* there!

"What's up, Hon?" Trish asked.

"I'm finding out all kinds of things about swingers and bisexuals and our neighbors."

"They couldn't teach us a *thing*!" she replied, leering at him.

He flipped off the computer. It was a great night.

Well, another day. Al took his coffee to the dock, Old Rocky was nowhere to be seen, the tape was still on the crime scene and someone was just getting into or out of a car across the canal. He heard the door slam. A minute later Levant came to stand looking around the area. He saw Al standing there and called, "Weird feeling, standing on the spot some dude gets croaked on!"

Then why stand there? Al thought, but he just called back,

"I suppose it would be."

Levant looked around and seemed to be trying to find something while looking like he was just casually looking over a crime scene, but soon waved and went back to his car to drive off. Al thought a minute, then grinned. He finished his coffee and went back into the house, decided that the cops had come at that time, so they would probably be at work and called. He got Norton.

"Sgt. Norton, I'm going to ask you a strange kind of question. I do have a reason, so please bear with me."

"So? Ask. Worst I'll do is say it's none of your business."

"I expect that's exactly what you'll do, but it's more to get you to look at something. What did you find that didn't quite fit over there?"

"Most of what we found over there didn't *quite* fit," Norton shot back. "What?"

"I don't know. There was someone over there this morning and I think he was looking for something he lost. It would be something small."

There was a silence, then, "We might have found one thing. Why?"

"Good. Is it something that can be tied to a specific person?"

"I don't think it would be ... it could, yes. Which person? I'll check it out myself, later. Kersey has already closed this case."

"Already!?"

"Mr. Rhamer, it's the kind of thing where we know for a fact it will never be prosecuted unless we accidentally find a solid connection with something else. I wish we could take the time, but we're shorthanded and underfunded as it is. We have to go after the ones we have a chance of proving in court. I didn't mean closed in the sense of closed. It's what we call a 'pending' case, which other cops know means we have some strong suspicions and it stinks from here to

Denmark, but we also know we don't have even a slim chance of proving.

"Maybe we've got the connection if what we found matches with a suspect and if we can get another connection of the suspect with the victim. With those two things, we'll re-open the case, at the least.

"So. Who?"

"Sam Levant."

"Thank you, Jesus! You don't know how I want it to be him! I'll check this out and let you know under the table, if you get the drift. When can I get there, after four, when he won't be around?"

"He goes out most nights, I think. He eats in restaurants, then goes to bars, I believe. If what you have checks out, I may have found a little something you can use to find a connection."

"Mr. Rhamer, you don't know how much, or why, I want to tag that bastard's ass!"

"I can imagine. Call me Al."

"Nort. Al, I think we can work together on this one. I think you want it solved. I know I do."

"But Kersey doesn't."

"No, Al. He does. He's got to be pragmatic about it. We don't have the resources. If we seem to be wasting a lot of time and taxpayers' money, we get replaced with someone who looks at everything as a bottom line issue. If there's too much hard question, drop it. Long investigations eat up the funds. Bottom line.

"Having said that. He'd rather find an easy solution and will bend things to that end."

"He gives up too easy," Al said. It wasn't a question. He said he'd call if he found anything else.

"Well, Love! It looks like we just might be able to do something about that body across the canal!" Al announced to Trish. "Remember, I told you Levant was looking for something over there?

"Seems he was, but the police already found it and didn't know where to connect it. I hope they do, now – or will before this time tomorrow"

"Just so you don't get involved in something nasty," Trish warned. "You're after a killer."

"Kind of adds a little excitement to life. I'll try to keep everything in perspective. I ain't suicidal."

He finished poking around, kissed Trish goodbye, and headed for work. He wondered what the cops had found that could be checked if Levant wasn't home. It had to be something outside, because they would have to get a warrant, if it wasn't.

Maybe something in his shed. Nort would have to be able to get in, though. It had a strong padlock, so that would take a warrant.

Al thought for a minute, then grinned. Maybe what they found was the kind of tool, like a common garden tool, that would make those wounds that looked like alligator bites. One of those claw things that you used to pull weeds. They were common enough, but it would mean they had to find the one used to get DNA or whatever from it.

Well, a piece of the tool, or they wouldn't need to find the rest of it in a specific place. A tine broken off and he would have the tool with a missing tine.

Wouldn't he have thrown it into the canal?

No. Not if people had seen him using it recently. He'd have to have one in his tools, in that case. One fished from the canal and his missing would be deadly.

Levant did a little gardening. Not so much, but he did have a lot of tools. He had been working on the annuals bed just last Sunday, so people would have seen him using it.

Really thin. Al didn't pretend to know what the cops would be looking for.

Another little item: If it was something like that, Levant

would have had to take it with him, which means a planned murder, which was murder one, which could get Old Sparky cranked up a few years down the road. Al liked the idea of Levant strapped to the chair.

Nort pulled into the drive at seven ten that evening and came to the door. Trish saw him coming and invited him in. Al was just finishing supper and there was plenty, if he cared for a bite or two. Nort could smell curry and he loved some curry, if it wasn't too hot.

It was almost like pizza! It was chopped curried pork with celery, tomatoes, bell pepper, onion and some other stuff on a thick pizza crust and was better than any pizza he'd ever tasted – and he loved pizza!

Trish said she'd give him the recipe for his wife, then he and Al took coffee out to the screened deck, looking over the canal.

"Okay," Nort began. "What we found was absolutely from Levant's place. You said you might have another connection?"

"Yes. Lubbock, Texas. What was it? A piece of the weed claw broke off?"

Nort looked puzzled. "Weed claw?"

"Yeah. The tool he used to kill him. I figure it was one of those claw things you use to pull weeds. He has all that kind of stuff."

"Cripes! Something that obvious, and we missed it? Cripes!

"He would have gotten rid of something like that, I suppose."

"He would have to explain where it had gone," Al answered, stubbornly. "If there was anything else, everyone in the neighborhood has seen him using the thing, so he couldn't not have it if you asked about it."

"Kee-rist!" Nort cried and took out his cell phone to tell

somebody named Andy to get a warrant started, very quietly, and said it was to search the properties of one Samuel Levant for a murder weapon. Probability was that keys discovered at the murder scene fit locks at Levant's place. The back door and a tool shed.

"If he knows you were there, he'll get rid of it," Al warned.

"I made very damned sure I wasn't seen there. I'm trained in that kind of thing. Nobody was home on the south house, there's nothing north or across the road, and I parked down toward the end and walked back to his place. I was only there two minutes to try the keys. I went back the same way."

Al nodded and grinned.

"We'll get the warrant first thing in the morning and, as the saying goes, descend on him like a swarm of killer bees. I'll need your other connections to make it stick, unless we can get irrefutable evidence at his place.

"You know, I think we might just do that! There's another little place he had to screw up somehow!"

"Yeah. His car. He carried the guy over there in his car."

"And he carried a bloody murder weapon in that same car when he left!" Nort said, triumphantly.

The cops showed up at Levant's place at 5:30AM and swarmed all over, as Nort had promised. A flatbed wrecker came to haul his car away and several tools were seized from his shed. The CSI team checked every inch of his house and took his computer in to search the hard drive. They found a weed claw, not in the shed ("*We* had the key to it, so he had to improvise!" Nort announced, later), but half buried in the bed of Mexican Petunias he had planted Sunday. They used a tool like those tree digger things, but smaller, to take the claw and the dirt around it without disturbing anything. Millie said she thought there would definitely be something there to get a DNA sample from.

"There was a washed plastic sheet on the fence," Kersey said, as they sat around Al's table drinking, for a change, very good coffee. Al had called in that he would be late. "I'd guess he carried the claw on it in the car, so there won't be anything in the car from that.

"We've got his ass, but good!"

"I don't know," Nort warned. "He looked very smug there. He's going to pull something. I can feel it."

"What can he pull?" Trish asked. "You have him!"

Al grinned, and said, "You know what? He's going to have an alibi that you can't break!"

"You mean that ... what? He didn't do it? Bull!" Kersey said.

"It's set up. You're supposed to find him and he can prove it was all planted. He was part of it, but there's something that is going to destroy everything you have. I think you can break it if you expect it."

"Yeah, if we expect it," Nort said. "We can counter it, if we can figure where it's going to come from."

"I think we probably can. Have Millie check every inch of

that car. Maybe check the Lexus again, very carefully. I think there's a very good chance a certain person's prints are somewhere in both cars!"

"Whose?" Nort asked.

"An old, dear friend from 'way back!"

"What's behind it? Do you know?" Kersey asked.

"I'd say blackmail. I wonder if Garner's married."

"Jeez! Who the hell is Garner?" Kersey demanded. "He the old friend from the past?"

"Uh-huh."

"Well, Mrs. Ames, I'm just glad we could resolve this problem for you," Al said, and grinned at his secretary, Alice Hunter, over the box of calendars sitting on his desk. "This is really kind of funny, in its own way. It's also why we try to have our clients handle this sort of thing. We aren't equipped, and Alf was just trying to help out a customer."

He listened for a moment and Alice rolled her eyes. Another agent had gone a long way past his job as a consultant to a shop owner to get her advertising printed. His job was to suggest the method and put her in touch with a good printer at a reasonable price, not to contract the job for her. Now the firm would have to pay for the botched job and get the job done right at their own expense. This was the third time Alf Rogers had overstepped his authority in his zeal to get the longest client list with resulting costs to the company.

Alf was a nice guy, but Al suspected he was an unemployed nice guy, as of this morning. The ad suggestion was for calendars featuring kittens at play. Alf had, as usual, been joking around with the printer's layout specialist and the calendars came with the theme of sex kittens at play. Hardly the way to advertise an antique shop!

"Oh, no! Mrs. Ames," Al lied. "I assure you, this was a mixup at the printers. I have Alf's layout right here and it's kittens playing with a ball of yarn on an antique Persian rug, not a sexy nude woman laying on a Persian rug! It says that in large, bold print! What?"

"Alf didn't call because he's attending a conference in Atlanta. I can assure you that, had he been here, he would be at that printer right now, reading them the riot act! We'll straighten this out, and you will have the calendars, the correct ones, by the first. As promised.

"We will, of course, pay for the whole silly mixup. All-Southern Associated Business Consultants accepts the responsibility, fully, though it actually is outside the services we offer. If one of our agents screws up, we make it right. Period."

"Thank you. I'm sure it will all work out. Have a good day!"

He hung up and shook his head. Alice looked at the calendar and laughed. She said she had done a fast design job using stock photos from the web, had the legal permissions and the printer was already producing the order. It was kittens superimposed over antiques and the Persian rug idea was one she would send in immediately to replace the January one of a kitten in a large Ming vase. It would be delivered before five.

His line buzzed and lit up. Alice reached across the desk to answer it, then handed Al the phone, saying, "Somebody named Nort? Personal?"

He nodded and took the receiver. "Hi, Nort! What's up?"

He listened for a minute, then said he had a problem there, but would see him in about an hour and a half. If it was all the same to him, just meet him at his house. There was nothing pressing at work, and he had already warned his partners that he would be tied up. Trish would make them a snack. He told Nort about the calendars and Nort said they would be fun to hang around at the station, so Al said he'd bring a few for him.

He called Trish and asked if she had something around to

make a snack, told her Nort would be with him and that he would be home for the day. He discussed the Yount account with Alice, made a few calls and headed home.

Nort said there was a big break, but they could use his help. Some odd fingerprints came from the cars. If they had been in only one car, it wouldn't mean anything, but they were in both cars as well as in Levant's house. They were also in Gorse's condo. That was the final point that made it very odd. Something sinister was going on here. They had to know whose prints those were and didn't have time to wait for Washington. They weren't in the local data base.

When Al drove into his driveway, Nort dropped in behind. They were talking by the cars when Trish called from the deck to say there was a call for Al that was supposed to be important. Al said he'd be right up and Nort asked if he had a recorder on the phone.

"I have a message machine that will record if I turn it on while I'm talking."

"I have a warning feeling. Would you mind? You can always erase it if it's nothing. I saw the caller ID readout there, so we'll know the caller's name and number."

They went upstairs and Al punched the "On" button to the machine when he took the receiver. The caller ID was blank, meaning it was from a blocked number. If it was a solicitor, they were going to get an ear full!

"Yes? Al Rhamer here."

"You back off or your lovely little wife is going to have an accident, got it?" came on in a gravelly man's voice. The line went dead.

Al stood there for a few seconds, getting madder and madder. When the machine was on, the voice came over the speakers and Nort was looking mad himself. Trish had a hand at her throat.

"Hon, get some stuff together. You're going to stay with your cousin for a few days!"

"Oh! I ... alright. Which one?"

"We'll decide after we're on our way to the airport. Well, Nort! Looks like whoever that was doesn't know me! I'll get anyone who threatens my family, and they're going to beg me to let them die!"

"Calm down!" Nort ordered sharply.

"Oh, I'm calm. I'm what you call deadly calm. I don't get any calmer than I am at this moment."

"I fixed some food," Trish said. "You can eat while I pack some stuff."

"I'm not hungry!" Al retorted.

"So? Eat anyway!"

"Yeah. Eat," Nort said. "This smells good! (Then in a very faint whisper) Al, I'm going to sneak someone into your house. We'll make some kind of distraction for them to get in. Okay?"

Al thought for a minute, then nodded. Nort took out his cell phone. He knew that wasn't tapped. He would also call from his car, not in the house. Al nodded again.

Everything was ready. Trish had her stuff in the car and they were standing there talking when Nort's cell phone vibrated. He casually turned it on and said, "Yeah?" There was no reply. He nodded at Al and Al and Trish got into their car as Nort got into his. Nort backed out of the driveway and across the street to "accidentally" run into the neighbor's mailbox. He stopped and got out and Al got out to look at it. Mrs. Carter came to look over her porch rail and Al called up to her that it was just knocked over and he'd put it back for her. She said it was in the wrong place, anyhow, so it would be a good time to move it to the other side of the drive. Al said he'd do it, because all it would take would be a post hole.

Al went into his garage and got his post hole digger, then he and Nort took about ten minutes moving the mailbox and setting it up right (actually, a little better than it had been). Everybody waved at everybody else and Al took the digger back to his garage. There were two police officers waiting in the garage. Al didn't see them get in there and he had been watching for them. He gave them a key to the upstairs and let one of them into the half-finished apartment downstairs. He then took Trisha to the airport. He noticed he was being followed only after a car had made the same turns he made from about a block back too many times for coincidence.

He was out of view on two of the turns, so knew there had to be a transponder hidden on his car.

He saw Kersey sitting across the shortterm lot in his own private car? With a woman inside?

The car that had followed him pulled into a space three rows down, behind some landscaping. He pointed to it for Kersey as soon as it was where he couldn't be seen and Kersey nodded. The woman got out of his car and waved frantically for Trish to come over. Al told her to get over there. Fast!

Trish was wearing a bright colored shawl, as was her custom, and the woman took it and almost shoved her into Kersey's car. Kersey waved and backed out as the woman came to Al, placing the shawl much like Trish wore it, but covering much of her face.

"Okay! Now we go get a flight and put me on a plane!" she said. "I'm Gloria Upton. Lt. Gloria Upton. We'll be followed into the terminal, so Bill will find the tracker on your car and we'll drop it by the speed bump when you leave. Go along to the west when you go out and he'll drop it as you pass the speed bump fifteen feet from where you're parked.

"Get the bags. Move!"

"What's going on?" Al demanded.

"Lord, I wish we knew! This thing has stirred something up, but what?"

They went into the terminal and to the AA desk. There was a flight to Miami in twelve minutes that had an available seat. Gloria flashed her badge and handed the clerk a note. The clerk looked scared and gave them a ticket. Gloria went through the security gate, acting insulted that the officer would look in her purse and being just a bit loud in decrying the way honest citizens were treated anymore.

She went into the flight tunnel and Al headed back toward his car. He noticed a heavy dark man who had been loitering to one side chose the same time to leave the terminal.

Al went to his car, backed out, went west and out of the gate. Nort was in an unmarked close and came alongside as he was going into the lot to toss Al a note. It said for him to go along the access road to the second right and turn there, go to the end and turn left onto the secondary road, then to go to 41 and to an address. And a "2"?

What the hell was going on? He had a few questions he wanted answers to before he went one inch further in this mess. What the hell was he involved in *now*?

He turned into the access road and a large van truck started out onto the main inlet a moment later, right in front of the car that had been following him. There was almost an accident and there were horns blowing and people getting out of the truck and car. Al saw that in his rearview mirror, then turned onto the secondary and headed for the address. It seemed Nort had arranged for his follower to lose him!

The address was a parking lot. He didn't know what else to do so pulled in, got a stub and parked on the second floor. Maybe that was what the "2" was about.

He sat in the car for a minute and a man came to show him a badge.

FBI?

"I'm Callaghan. Leave your car right here. You can use the one I'm driving for awhile, then come back for yours to go home tonight.

"I suppose you have some questions."

"You suppose right!"

"We'll go to HQ. You'll get as much as we can give you there. That Norton character is sharp! I think we'll end up offering him a job as an agent!"

"I seriously doubt he'd take it. He seems reasonably intelligent. What am I involved in – and how the *hell* did it happen?"

"You did it to yourself," Callaghan said, grinning at him. "I suppose Norton is smarter than to take the job, too. It's not anywhere nearly all it's cracked up to be on TV."

They drove the three year old Toyota to a somewhat decrepit house in an "affordable" neighborhood, where Callaghan told him to come on inside. He introduced Al to "Bill" and that was all he needed to know.

"Not by a hell of a long shot! I've got a *lot* of questions and I intend to get answers! This crap has gone as far as it's going unless I *do* get those answers! The big bad FBI isn't going to intimidate me, I can guaran-goddamned-tee you!"

"You, I kinda like," Bill said. "Believe it or not, we're trying to protect you and your wife. You've rocked a boat that wasn't yet ready to be rocked. That could be good or bad. It'll be what we can make it.

"So. Ask your questions.

"I'll start by telling you it's about an international ring of blackmailers who are financing little warlords in Central Africa."

"In ... Central Africa? Not in Iraq or wherever?"

"There's a place in Africa where some people found a large lode of uranium about ten years ago. If certain little tin warlords get control, places like Iran will have a very easy source of the stuff. They get that quantity and the whole area is badly destabilized and under threat of nuclear war."

"Oh, give me a damned break! How could that area possibly be more destabilized than it is right now, and that from our own idiotic meddling!"

"I won't argue the point. I have to agree it's bad. We're getting a lot of pressure. Somebody else wants control of that uranium. They do *not* want it to fall into Iran's hands."

Al thought a minute, then said, "So! Where does Levant's income fit into this? He doesn't do anything but lay around being obnoxious, yet he has that car and house and he always seems to have money."

"You see our problem," Bill said.

"I do?" Al was completely lost now.

"WHY, DAMNIT!" Bill yelled. "WHY the HELL is Israel backing up this blackmail ring and working so hard to put that uranium into Iran's hands? It doesn't make any damned *sense*!"

"It does, unless you deliberately refuse to see it. So! Where is Trish? If anything happens to her, I'm coming after you, the FBI, Israel, and anybody else who gets in my way! You'll get me, but I'll damned well get a few of you first, and I'll see that you don't have a secret left! Maybe I can figure a few angles myself."

Bill laughed. "We found that stuff you had ready to go out on the net if you don't cancel it at specific times. It's cancelled."

"Yes. Wasn't that just so very easy?" Al shot back sweetly, smirking at him. Bill studied him carefully, eyes narrowed. The silence drew out, then Bill shook his head.

"So. Do we understand one another?" Al asked.

"You don't have a clue as to what you're letting yourself in for. Okay. Ask. I'll answer everything I can. No more bull crap. Promise."

"Trish?"

"She's a guest of Norton. He likes her. His wife, Jeanne, is a jewel. She's safe there, more than anywhere we could come up with. Nobody would suspect she was taken there. Gloria got her bags and another cop took them to her."

"Gorse?"

"Contact man. Let his personal penchant for blackmailing extend to others on a more personal level. He ran a gay bar, as you discovered, and started the whole thing 'way back when. It grew into what it is today when some bigshit diplomats from that country were visiting Texas to study farming methods. They put him into contact with people who put him into contact with people who.

"He didn't know when to stop. I mean, a hundred bucks a month to keep mum about an affair between two men who were married at the time."

"No kidding? Levant and Garner?"

"Jeez! You've connected Garner already? They kept that low-key to where it took us five damned years to find the connection between them! Levant and Garner didn't communicate in any way!"

"Oh? And Garner moved to Orlando just after Gorse moved here? Garner had the connection with both of them since the UFO thing, and you didn't connect that? It took about fifteen minutes to find that from the web. It was Garner's prints that were found everywhere they shouldn't have been?"

"No. Samuels. He's tied in and is a pro hit man. He seems to have disappeared."

"Terrorist suspect?"

"Ain't the Patriot Act a total hoot? Garner's too smart to leave any connections around to find, and we don't have any idea how he and Levant communicate."

"You have a habit of overlooking the obvious," Al pointed out. "Levant go to the library much? To comp cafes?"

Bill looked interested, then thoughtful, then tired. "So obvious. Set up an anonymous e-mail account and only access it in the public web connections. We would have found that, I'm sure."

"Did you check Levant's hard drive carefully?"

"What?"

"Did Levant make up stories and send them to the web mags? I heard he did that. From Gladys Forbes, who said she saw him writing one, once."

"Jeez! There weren't any mags. Just web addresses. We can't keep up with this computer shit!"

"So. Break the code they used."

"But he didn't get any ... don't say it. He didn't get any replies *on his home computer*."

"How about we lose the idea of making Norton an agent and make you one?"

"Okay. When, as the old saying goes, there's a fullscale blizzard decimating hell!"

"That's what Norton's going to say. So! Next question? I'm learning more from your questions that you ever will from my answers!"

Al laughed. "Oh, I've learned something!"

"Like we're nothing more than a bunch of Keystone Kop incompetents?"

"I already knew that! I learned that something very big is going on here. It isn't about any uranium in Africa."

"No. That's very real," Bill said, seriously. "It's just not all of it. I can't and won't tell you the rest. Not yet. I think someday you'll have the right to know."

"Okay. Fair enough. State or national? Both?"

Bill stared at him a minute, then shook his head.

"Anything that stinks as bad as this crap has to be politically driven. It has to be from 'way up the ladder, too. That's possibly state and probably national ... and possibly international. I think I see."

"Then I wish you'd clue *me*! This thing doesn't make any sense, no matter how you slice it! It's a bunch of nutzos!"

"*There's* a point on which I have to agree, but very dangerous nutzos. It isn't obvious to you?"

"Maybe it's supposed to be so obvious, I think I see where you're going with this. Israel wouldn't take that chance."

"What chance? The chance to draw US into a nuclear war? The chance to sucker us one more time?"

"Look, your wife's a Muslim, so you tend to have your viewpoint skewed. Israel is in a bad spot."

"First off, my wife's an Episcopalian and not a devout one. Second, Israel is exactly in the spot they put themselves. It's partly our fault, because we back them up when the whole world can see what's going on, except for us, but Israel is the one that insists on treating everyone else like they were Nazis and the rest of the world are Jews. We've become a Mussolini to the present regime there. They cry about the horrible atrocities they suffered, then do the exact same things to the Palestinians. Their only defense is that the Nazis did it to all Jews and they only do it to a few. We're supposed to make atrocities a matter of numbers now?

"Let's not get off on that. It won't lead anywhere.

"What we have to know now is which one is pulling the strings here. It's either Garner or Levant, and Levant is the one who doesn't seem to need a job, while Garner has to make a living. That could be a set up.

"Wait a minute! What you said about ... Levant was married?"

"He still is. They've been legally separated for more than ten years. He talks to her once a month when he visits their fourteen year old brat. And she is a *brat* if there ever was one!"

Al couldn't help but break out laughing. Bill was giving him a very strange look.

"Well, I'd better head back home. I just leave the rattletrap where I'm parked?"

"First, what's the joke?"

"Have you checked the hard drive of the little missus?"

"I will be dog-*damned*! Why do we always miss the obvious? We get so tied up in trying to figure how they do something in some clever way and it's the purloined letter every damned time! Damn! They use a code, but work it through her so there's never a connection."

"It's just a little too easy," Al warned. Bill nodded.

$$\underline{1 + 1 = 4}$$

Al pulled into his drive and went directly upstairs. There were no lights and the place was quiet. The officer there stepped out of the bathroom into the hall, nodded and stepped back. He didn't say anything, so Al knew they suspected the house was bugged and didn't want to give themselves away. He turned on the CD player. Trish had *Dark Side of the Moon* by Pink Floyd in it. He liked it, so turned it up a bit.

He went to the refrigerator and took out the rest of the pizza, cut up some lettuce and tomatoes, noticed there was a cucumber, so diced that into the salad and added some of the dressing Trish made. There was a lot more than one person could eat. He made iced tea and put part of the meal on a tray to take to the cop in the bathroom. That seemed to surprise him and he nodded his thanks. Al pointed to the downstairs, but the cop shook his head.

Well, it would probably seem weird if he were to take a tray of food downstairs.

He got on the phone with the business for an hour or so. The calendar bit was settled and everyone was happy now. There were several hang-up calls to his personal line. When the machine answered, the caller hung up and the time was noted, but that was all.

Someone wanted to know where he was. Maybe someone who had been following him and had lost him?

He watched CSI Miami and Without a Trace, then took a shower and went to bed. The cop stepped out of the bath without a word when he went in. When he got up in the morning the cops were gone. He hadn't heard a thing!

He had his regular morning coffee on the dock. Keep the routine. Old Rocky was there, lazing on the top. He seemed to be staying around more than usual.

Norton drove into the drive and came down to the dock.

He said, very low, to be careful what they said, because there were ways to hear anything said from half a mile away. His wife was doing fine and was adjusting to him working odd hours on this one.

That meant Trish and Nort's wife were getting along well and that it wasn't any bother to them. Al knew Trish would fit right into anything.

"I'm going to work today," Al announced. "I can't let this kind of thing interfere with the company. I don't even know what's going on, and I'm pissed because Trish is at her cousin's (Nort shook his head) in Daytona or somewhere. She went to Miami, but she said she wouldn't stay there. It's best if I don't know where she is.

"Nort, this is driving me batshit! I don't know what's happening anymore! All I wanted to do was find out who trashed some tourist. Now there's some gay gang from Texas involved or something! It's crazy!"

Nort grinned slightly to let him know he'd pulled that one back out very nicely, thank you! "I think it has something to do with Al Queda, personally. Maybe Iraq or Syria. Some creep from the FBI was asking us for the case files, so that's a hell of a red flag! I'm a bit more than slightly interested because the ass said we didn't find it and that was a relief! There's something there to find, Al. I'm going to be cut off of the case because Levant's caught. I think he expects someone to get him off, the way he's acting.

"Well, one good thing about the case. I like you and your wife. I'll be glad when Levant's put away so she can come back home. I want her to give my wife some of her recipes.

"I'm supposed to be looking for someone who saw a black Ford truck the night of the murder. I don't even know where that came from, except it's supposed to be some killer for hire who was around. It may mean Levant hired somebody to kill Gorse, but he's guilty as hell, either way, and we won't find some professional hit man from Chicago or wherever. I'll probably see you later if I find anything."

Al nodded and walked back to the house with him, then took his cup upstairs while Nort drove off. What they'd said there would leave the impression they thought they had the case sewed up to any listeners who knew the true story and the one they were trying to plant.

He went to his car to head for the office. There was a note on the front seat. Nort wanted to meet him at the Longhorn Restaurant near his office at 11:00. He might be a few minutes, so wait for him.

That didn't seem right. Nort wouldn't put a note in his car because he would have to be seen doing it. Al grinned and headed for the office. He stopped on the way at Office Max and bought a throwaway cell phone with a thousand minutes on it. He used it to call Kersey and explained what had happened. Kersey could get word to Nort. Al was to go to the Longhorn to see who he did see.

"If I'm at the Longhorn, I won't be home or at my office, will I?" Al asked. Kersey chuckled and said Al was sharp. He was planning on having someone both places.

"You almost had a visitor last night, but he got spooked," Kersey said. "I think maybe I could say *she* got spooked, but we're not sure."

"That's why the cops were gone so early this morning?"

"Uh-huh."

"You didn't think he or she would try it again?"

"No. Spooked is spooked. They're waiting until you're seen at the Longhorn. Larry says you're one hell of a cook. You gave him some kind of stuff like he never tasted before and it was *good*!"

"Nort ate some of it yesterday. That was leftovers and a salad."

"You're calling here, so you've arranged to not be tapped?" Kersey asked.

"Yeah. I got a throwaway."

"Call five five five four four three four and ask for Bill. You're supposed to know what that means."

"Okay. He's FBI."

"Bull crap!" Kersey snapped. "Catch you later." He hung up. Al punched the number. Bill answered the second ring.

"I'm supposed to call you?"

"Yeah. Levant's wife took the brat to ice skating practice before daylight and we sort of went in her house. We have a whiz on comps who took about two minutes to record everything on her hard drive and he took it to the lab. Seems Levant was sending crap to her since she got the comp three years ago, at least. So was Garner."

"And?"

"What?"

"No games. They were sending the stuff to her, so how was she getting it to them? When Levant went to see the brat is obvious, for him, but what about Garner? How did she contact him?"

"That seems to be the rub. She didn't, and she arranged to drop the girl off and pick her up where she didn't even see Levant. If the girl was being used as a courier, she didn't have a printout or anything. None were made from that comp. She doesn't even have a printer."

"Then she was using the internet. That means there's another one or two involved, somehow. Check her e-mail address book."

"Yeah. They're doing that. There's somebody else in this. We had Garner and Levant, then Levant's wife, now somebody else. Start with one, add another and we're already up to at least four, probably five!

"Al, they are *not* sending it to his comp! I really don't think they're sending it to him, anywhere, because there would be a trace. The hidden e-mail from the public terminals won't work with more than two!

"What is the ... I mean, who ... I don't know what I mean.

We're up against a genius, I'm afraid."

"To tell the truth, I think you're up against the one thing that beats a genius every time. I think you're up against a normal intelligence who's what I call 'born lucky.' There's no way around that!

"I have to get to work. I'll leave the math to you."

"Math?"

"How one plus one can equal four."

Al went to a seat behind a palm where he could see the whole front section of the restaurant and who came and went. He had called Nort, but was told he was on a case that came up just half an hour before east of Bonita Springs.

Uh-huh. He was sure Nort fell for that one.

No one he recognized, except for clients and people who worked in the area and came in regularly, came in for almost an hour, so he went back to the office where the rest of the day went without much new happening. He caught up with things, then headed home. He was missing Trish, but would have to suck it up and live with it. Bill was right that he'd brought it on his own head.

Everything seemed normal until he looked close. Little things were a bit out of place. Things were moved the least little bit. He thought of calling Nort, then thought better of it. The best thing would be to not appear too close to him. Someone might get suspicious if there was too much contact.

He was at a loss for occupying his time, so did some paperwork and watched as much TV as he could stand. It was unbelievable how much mindless crap was on the tube that was designed for teenagers.

Well, they were a big market, but not as big as a couple of years ago.

He finally went to bed.

"Hi, Al, just calling to see how things are going," Nort

greeted. "I'm having coffee and donuts at the shop just south of the station and figured I'd call to tell you that Levant has an airtight alibi, but you knew that.

"Didn't wake you, did I? You said you're always up early."

Al started to say something, then saw what Nort was saying. Meet him at the donut shop. "I'm awake, but just laying here. I'm 'way behind at the office, so I guess I'll go in early. I really miss Trish. I'm mostly just wandering around feeling sorry for myself."

"Hmm. Well, I'll call again if we find anything. We're getting some kind of interference from over our heads. Someone wants us to back off. It's someone with influence.

"Maybe I'll come over on the weekend. Fishing any good in that canal?"

"Not very. We can go out in the boat. It's a way to relax as much as I can with Trish not here." They chatted a few minutes, then Al hung up, got dressed, and headed for the office. He saw a car pull out about two blocks behind him when he left the house. It wasn't a car from that neighborhood. It could be the cops or the FBI or something else. He was taking no further chances. There was probably another transponder on his car, by now.

He went into the office, turned on some lights and left a note for Alice to call a few clients if he wasn't back by regular opening time, then went out the service entrance to the alley in back, got a company car, and drove out toward the trail to find the same car was following him, so there was either another transponder on the company car or someone figured he might do that.

He pulled into the parking lot at Home Depot and went inside before the follower was where he could see who got out of the car. There was no way he was seen getting into it.

He went out the garden shop side gate and crossed Gladiolus to the Wal*Mart lot, where there was always a cab or two. He got in one and rode to the donut shop. Nort asked what took him so long, and he explained.

"Well, seems we've run into a dead end with our info disbursement trace," Nort said. "I can't figure out how it gets from the ex to whoever gets it to Levant and Garner. It's a cell-type deal that has a circle built in, somehow."

"Somebody gives it to somebody else who gives it to another, then it gets back through another one. Garner's in Orlando and Levant's here, so they aren't getting any ... but maybe they are! Same person contacts Levant and Garner.

"Or not. A real mess, huh?"

"Yeah! If you're into understatement. We'll have to get every e-mail address from all of them and try to track them down. The bad thing is, it's not legal, really, and we can't get some of them."

Al nodded, then took out his throwaway cell to call Bill, who he got out of bed.

"Did you get the hard drive readouts from the ex Mrs. Levant and from Garner?" Al asked, without preamble.

"Yeah. Why?"

"Did you get all the e-mail addresses they use regularly?"

"I see where you're going. Yeah. We're checking them all out. That takes a special kind of skill. You can get as many e-mail addresses as you want. There are dozens of those free carriers. We can trace most of them. Some people use three or four servers, too, so it can get pretty complicated. It will take a few days."

"Will you give me a list?"

"Hell no! Who do you think you are? You know very well that I can't give you that kind of information!

"Of course, I may want to leave a note for you in your car and accidentally leave the wrong one."

"Not in the car. It seems everybody and his dog is putting odd little things in and on that damned car! It's got another transponder. I had a hard time giving that turkey following me the slip. Not your man is it?"

"No. Al, you be careful! These are some very nasty and extremely dangerous people. An amateur investigator is almost sure to end up a dead amateur investigator."

"I intend to be low-key, all the way. You could drop by the office and give Alice some forms about the crime reports or something and a certain list could have been in the envelope you never even knew was there because some damned *clerk* didn't label the envelope and you thought that's what it was there on your desk *for* and you just can't get help who know their asshole from a cow turd anymore!"

"Or something."

Al got up, fixed breakfast and went to the dock with his coffee. Old Rocky was down toward the west end of the canal. Landon was getting his boat ready to go out in the bay.

Damn it! He wanted Trish back home!

"Want to go out?" Landon called.

Why the hell not? He was planning to go out and take Nort in his boat, but Nort had to work the weekend on special assignment.

"I need to do something!" Al called back. "Gulf or bay?"

"Pompano should be running about now. Gulf! Half an hour?"

"Good enough!" Al finished his coffee and got his tackle. He should mow the lawn, but he would do that tomorrow. He'd just screw around today, like he did most Saturdays, and work in the yard tomorrow.

Landon came to his dock, they got in the boat and headed out the canal. Todd and Lucy were just heading out and they yelled back and forth until they were in the bay. Todd and Lucy were going to mostly fool around the pass and the barrier islands.

Paul Arnstein, from Pelican Perch, was going out with his wife and they stopped and chatted for a few minutes. Paul and Landon had been friends since they both moved to the area at the same time.

Al looked for someone to be following him, but supposed they didn't have a boat handy, so would wait until he came back. It did seem a little odd that they hadn't even considered that. He *was* planning to take Nort out, after all!

Maybe they were losing interest in him. He could hope.

Four nice pompano for the freezer and a trout for supper. He would fix it like Trish often did, with a little butter, soya sauce and cumin and bake it. They'd come in about 4:30 and had almost hit Old Rocky, who was swimming lazily out of the canal mouth into the bay. He would be gone for a couple of months, now. He probably went up the river when he wasn't in the canal. Al would miss having him floating there during his morning coffee.

Levant was home. His car was in his drive.

Al checked the door to the downstairs. He had put a small chip of wood near the edge of the sill and it was gone, so the door had been opened. He didn't have a clue as to what they expected to find there. He supposed he'd find they'd been upstairs, too. He grinned and almost called Bill on the throwaway, but noticed it was not quite exactly where he'd left it. It was only moved about a quarter inch, but he'd left it where he couldn't see the page number of the open book it was laying on. Now he could.

What did they expect to find with him? He didn't know anything!

Maybe they wanted to know if Nort had learned anything and would tell him, or maybe they thought he'd call Trish on it and they'd know where she was. He knew something, but couldn't figure what. There was something he knew that was deadly dangerous to them.

He sighed. There was some time before dark, so he got out the mower and did the lawn. He would trim and pull the weeds tomorrow.

His throwaway rang and he answered with, "Al Rhamer here. Talk on about anything you want the world to know! That you Trish? Where are you?"

That would tell either Bill or Nort, the only two who knew that number, something was up.

"Mr. Rhamer? Norton here. You will remember, I promised to keep you abreast of the case of the body you found, and I wanted to tell you that Mr. Levant has been cleared. He was with some people who can say with dead certainty that he was nowhere near that area at the time the crime was being committed."

Al felt devilish. "Oh? I don't understand? Didn't he say, standing right there in the lot, that he had come home about that time and didn't see any lights over there? How could anyone say he wasn't in the area? It's about three hundred fifty feet from the road to where the body was. Call me Al."

He could hear the suppressed laughter in Nort's voice. "That struck me, also, Mr. Rhamer. Al. It would appear he was lying when he said that, or he was lying when he said he was with those other people, so he was lying, no matter what. The only thing is, he was very definitely with those people, so was not there to not see any lights."

"He's an ass! Probably so drunk he didn't know where he was. People who stay out until all hours every night have to be drinking or worse. Oh! That bar! He wasn't with a gay crowd, was he?"

"Yes."

"Can you believe them, then?" Al asked, innocently. "It's pretty plain Levant doesn't mind using blackmail from the same sources where you found out about the gay bar and affairs." He hoped Levant was the one listening to the conversation!

"Well, a policeman was called to a disturbance at the bar and has identified Levant as one of the people there."

"I see. Very convenient," Al replied, drily.

"Yes. Isn't it? Anyhow, I suppose I'll grab a bite and go home. I'm at the end of a shift and a half and am just plain worn out. Be glad you're not a cop.

"You wouldn't happen to have any of that pizza stuff left over, would you? Hint! Hint!"

Al laughed. "No, but I can make some in fifteen minutes. I have the sauce. All I have to do is make the dough and bake it. I was going to fix fish, but that's easier. Come on over. You are no substitute for my wife, but at least you're somebody to talk to. I'm going stir crazy here."

"My wife's in Miami, at her mother's place, and I have a bigscreen and the Heat is playing on cable. Why not come over, bring the stuff and bake it at my place? You can crash on the couch if the game plays late.

"I think you can see I think we'll be friends when this mess is over. It might already be. We're getting pressure to drop it."

"Kersey said something like that. I wonder what's really going on."

"Want the truth? Better than fifty percent, we'll never know. See you in three quarters of an hour at my place?"

"Yes. Fine with me. You'll have to tell me where it is. All I know is you're called Nort and you live in Golden Gate."

Nort laughed and gave him instructions on how to find the place.

Well! Nort had arranged for him to be with his wife! He owed him for that!

"Oh! Old Rocky's gone," Al said to Trish, as they were finishing the homemade butterscotch pudding she made. "Landon and I went fishing, and he was down at the bay when we came in."

"I guess that'll shut that bunch up who want us to catch him and kill him. It doesn't matter to that bunch of looneys that the damned gator didn't have anything to do with any of it."

"Oh, Rock's a fixture. There's no way anyone in the neighborhood would let you bother him," Trish said. "Al, Nort and Jeanne are more fun than you could imagine! Jeanne will be back tomorrow night and she fixes me up to look like a cheap Latino slut and we go to the bar and have a red wine. She tells them I'm her cousin's wife. The cousin who is a bigtime drug lord who will cut the balls off anyone who looks at his wife crooked. I look like a common cheap bar whore and they'd better not even look at me! It's great fun!"

"It won't be any fun if one of them decides to waylay you somewhere!" Al warned.

"Those people are terrified of Alonzo," Nort said. "He's actually an undercover narc who works for us and he's posed as Jeanne's cousin for a long time. Those six they found executed and castrated about a year ago, he sort of let's them think they were punks who made a pass at his girlfriend. The skinny's always been that his wife is one *hot* broad who he keeps out of sight of anyone because he's so jealous he might fly into a rage. If he'll execute five cruds for making a pass at his girlfriend, think what he might do if it's his *wife*!"

"Oh? *Did* he execute them?" Trish asked, grinning impishly.

"I wish!" Nort said, with feeling. "We'd have a wee tiny chance of solving that! Druggie executions? Forget it! Whoever did that is probably in Peru or Colombia or some-where!"

They had a good time and Al and Trish slept in the guest room. He went home about four in the morning. He took his coffee to the dock. It just wasn't the same without Rocky floating there.

Al got off work at five and was home at five twenty five. There were several police cruisers and Millie's big lab van in front of Levant's. Maybe they broke down his alibi, but Millie wouldn't be there for that, would she?

Kersey was in front, talking to a uniformed cop, saw Al and waved. Al walked up the road to ask him what was going on. Levant's alibi crashed?

"No, it's solid. Levant crashed. His throat's been cut," Kersey said. "I suppose you'll have an ironclad, so we won't get you for this one, but, sooner or later, we'll tag your ass! I'll get you! Count on it!"

Al laughed. "Ocifer! I wash drivin' down the street jush mindin' my own (hic) bishness when that mailbox *ashtacked* me!

"Making jokes at murder scenes now? Shows how much he'll be missed."

Al's throwaway buzzed. He turned it on and said, "Don't say anything! You'll give me away!" That would tell Bill, if it wasn't Nort, that the line was being listened to. "What? Al Rhamer here."

"Looks like another 'why'," Bill said. "This one's even screwier than the other. Call me when you get a minute or two. Just chat." He didn't identify himself, so any listener wouldn't know who he was. "I'm going nuts, wandering around this apartment with nothing to do. TV is smelly crap!

"Women! You can guess Veronica walked out on me. Again! Shit! Didn't even say *why*! Dingy broad!"

"Yeah, Jack. When I have some time. I'm sort of busy right now. Catch you later." He turned it off. Kersey raised an eyebrow.

"Dumb-ass! He wants me to listen to him whine and moan about how another woman dumped him, and just because he was oh so innocently chatting with some other woman, in bed, in her place."

Kersey mouthed, "Bill? FBI?" and Al nodded very slightly. Kersey knew his phone was tapped, somehow. "Keep your women problems to yourself! I have my own stupid crap to live with!" With some of those modern listening devices there could be something focused on them right now. This was a lot bigger than Al had ever considered, if they were going to such extremes, and Bill and Kersey were keeping together on it.

"I don't want to hear it. If you play the game, you pay the ticket. So! Levant's gone, so you might never find the connections, huh?"

"You're an unusually intelligent person, Al," Kersey said, seriously. "Ninety nine percent of the people I come across in murder cases, I won't give the time of day. Because they'll screw it up. This one, there's some kind of connection 'way over my head, and we're getting heavy pressure to back off. It could be coming from Homeland Security, the FBI, CIA ... who knows?

"Al, there's someone checking on you. We've been watching your place ever since you got that threat Nort overheard. Three separate people have gone in when you weren't around. It could be our guys, but it might not be. If you know anything at all, I *have* to know it, too! It's to your *own* advantage to tell me!"

This was to try to get him off the hook.

"Damn it all! I don't have a *clue*! I don't know what the *hell* is going on! All I did was report a damned body across the canal! Now there's some kind of weird connection with terrorists or something as stupid and I don't ... it doesn't have anything to do with me! Kersey, I don't *know* anything! I swear!"

Kersey shook his head and nodded. "Be damned careful. Be very, very, damned careful. Somebody *thinks* you know something, and that's the same as if you did, to them."

Al nodded.

Bill had been right about one thing. TV was pure smelly crap! Al was going to be wandering around the house, himself. He couldn't call Bill, because there was nowhere he wouldn't be heard there, and to go anywhere would be out of character.

No it wouldn't! Trish wasn't there to do the regular shopping! He could find ten reasons to go to the grocery store!

He went to the cabinet, looked over the stuff there (knowing that whoever had searched the house would know if he had most things) and started taking things out to fix supper. He had the fish almost ready to put in the oven, so would need soya sauce and cumin. There wasn't any ground cumin (there was in the storeroom, but he might not know that, seeing it was something Trish would keep stocked). He swore and looked in the next cabinet.

He couldn't go for only cumin. That would be much too suspicious.

He was getting low on coffee. There was just one egg. The bread was getting stale. There was no celery (might as well make a list and get things they would need).

He wrote out a list, sighed, put the fish back in the refrigerator, and went to his car. Publix was only a couple of miles away, so he went there to get the stuff. He managed to give the dark man who had been at the airport to watch him the slip in the freezer section by going across to the wine display when he was in the next isle with the freezer case between them, then, leaving the cart there, he slipped out the door to the stockroom, went out the loading deck and around to the pay phone, called Bill, learned that not very much was new and that there was some kind of solid connection with someone in the neighborhood, found through the computer e-mail links, but they couldn't pinpoint it. Bill warned him about using the computer for anything sensitive.

"I have a way around that, except it's on my phone line. I can handle any e-mail contact you like, with no record. Dial-up, of course."

"Like hell! Don't get cute or you'll end up just like like Levant! Modern computers, you can find anything! There's absolutely no way to completely erase anything! It's on the drive and it can be taken *off* the drive!"

"Yeah. That's the trouble with modern computers. I better get back inside. My follower will be getting suspicious by now."

"That easy to spot?"

"If I hadn't seen him at the airport, he would be almost impossible. I *did* see him there, so it's pretty obvious."

Bill laughed and Al hung up and went back through the stockroom. The follower was by his cart, looking around for him. There were rest rooms by the stockroom entrance for the employees. Al slipped into the door, then made a small noise by kicking a cardboard box beside the door as he came out and went to his cart. The follower grabbed a bottle of Merlot and moved on down the isle. Al didn't seem to notice him, talked to a woman about the best wine to serve with Beef Bourdelaise (none), and went to checkout. As he went out the section where the carts were kept, a boy and girl in Publix uniforms were coming in the door holding hands. As soon as they saw him, they almost jumped apart and the girl said, "You screw up an order like that again and you're history!" as they walked past him.

Ah! Young love! Don't let the supervisor know the employees are fraternizing!

So! *That* was it! Al suddenly knew what it was he knew! It was the last thing he would have guessed!

"Nort? Al here.

"Listen, Nort, I'm getting worried about my wife. I don't know where she is and haven't heard from her. She ... Nort, she's missing, as far as I know! Can you try to find her for me?"

Nort would know something important was up. "I can't, because I'm on assignment.

"Tell you what. Come in and file a regular MP report, I'll handle it and we can put our best man, or best woman, in this case, on it. I can't investigate it, but I can damned well see the right person gets the case. You can fill out the form in ten minutes, so come on in before you go to work and I'll be here to take your statement."

"Thanks, Nort. You don't know how worried I'm getting. I thought she'd find a way to call or something by now. I'll see you in about half an hour."

He hung up. That would be a good excuse for him to go to the station. They certainly wouldn't be overheard there!

He got dressed as quickly as he could, got in his car, and headed for the police station. Nort, Kersey and Bill were waiting for him. "I figure you've found what you know, so I called these two clowns," Nort greeted.

"I also want to know what you meant about getting around the e-mail trace thing," Kersey said. "Coffee? It's pretty disgusting."

"I'll try it. I think I know your link, which means who Levant's killer is, if not Gorse's. I'll give you what I know in chronological order and see if you figure it the same way I do."

"You give us the missing link there and we'll automatically figure it out," Bill said.

"Jeez! This stuff really *is* disgusting!" Al cried, and sat.

"Let's see what I have and how it works.

"First, I've lived here for twelve years. The Forbes and the Goodalls were already there. Carter moved in a year later, across the street. Levant came just about a month after them. Watson, Knight, Haverty, and Collins all moved in since, but they're just people who wave at each other and us if they happen to see us outside.

"I reasoned that Levant's contact would have to be someone who was already there or someone who moved in almost immediately after he did. That's nobody, which only leaves Forbes, Goodall, Carter, and me.

"It isn't Carter. He's an invalid, and she's never in contact with any of us, except to wave and talk in the yard now and then.

"Forbes is obvious. Gladys. She was with him fairly often. I imagine you've checked her out thoroughly and that you haven't found anything, which leaves Goodall."

"No," Bill said. "We've checked them out. It is *not* them. I know that from another angle. In addition, they don't own a computer and haven't been observed using one. Ever. You figured it wrong."

"I knew it wasn't them! Let me finish!

"When I first met them, they came to welcome me into the neighborhood. They're very normal middle-class people with nothing to hide. I even did a little work for him at my company. When I first met the Carters was when I went to welcome them to the neighborhood. When I first met the Forbes was when they stopped in their boat on their way out fishing. Old Rocky was sitting there and they explained he had been around before they moved in and was a local fixture. They explained how he would come around, stay a couple of weeks, then disappear for a month or more. Landon invited me to go fishing with him because Gladys didn't really enjoy the boat, and he needed a fishing buddy.

"He was slightly ... pompous, I guess you'd say. She was

obviously a snob. Him, I liked. Her, I didn't.

"I met Levant when he was moving in. He stopped in his car while I was mowing out front and said he was moving in and blah, blah, blah. I saw from early on that he wasn't the type who anyone was going to hang with. There was something about him that wasn't very likeable. It's kind of strange, but the first thing I thought when he was driving away was that he and Gladys would probably get along.

"The next time I saw him was when I was going out to get the paper one morning. I heard voices in the empty lot west of my place behind that big silverthorn bush and stepped around to find him and Landon talking about something. They both seemed embarrassed, for some reason, but I didn't think anything of it.

"I saw Gladys at his house, or her car, several times, and Landon seemed to suddenly develop a dislike for him. I figured Landon thought there was some hanky-panky with his wife and considered it none of my business.

"I did note that I was being followed everywhere I went, but I doubt they knew I'd spotted the tail. I was followed everywhere, except when I went out fishing with Landon. I was shopping at Publix last night and, as I was leaving, a boy and girl were coming in. They were holding hands and giggling. Both had on the Publix uniform shirts. They saw me and she was suddenly grinding on him for a botched order or something and threatened to have him fired.

"I told myself, 'Ahha! If their boss finds out they're fraternizing, they both get canned on the spot!' It hit me right there and then that..."

"Cripes! *Landon Forbes?!*" Bill cried. "I said you were smarter than the bunch of us, and that you'd figure it out ... the part about you knowing something you didn't know you knew.

"Okay. There isn't any traffic from their computer, but he's gone a lot ... but ... so it's both of them. I wonder! Are they the top dogs?"

"No way!" Kersey cried. "I don't see that at all!"

"They're probably the contact point for the area and are probably as high as it goes here," Nort said. "How do they work it, Al?"

"Bill, you've checked their place over? I mean, the whole place?"

"Yuh."

"Do they happen to have an old computer around? I mean, pre-ninety?"

"Gimme a sec," Bill replied and took out his cell to call the office. He said to fax a complete list ... and he meant *complete* ... of everything they found at the Forbes place. He gave them the fax number at the station. They sat around chatting until the list came through. There was an old IBM and an old Tandy in the garage in plastic bags. Both had external modems.

Al smirked. "Now I'll tell you how to send and receive e-mails without any record anywhere."

Bill grinned and shook his head. Nort and Kersey looked puzzled.

"You send it to and from an old dinosaur comp that doesn't *have* a hard drive, in the modern sense!" Bill said, triumphantly. "You use a comp from back when DOS meant DOS. The most you had in the permanent memory was the MS-DOS boot and maybe a basic load program!"

"But ... it won't work!" Kersey cried. "The damned banner on the server would take more space than the thing could hold!"

"Not if you and the other party used only a basic program without graphics or images and you ran the e-mail directly to an old three point five floppy, Al pointed out You could send and receive a book in text only!"

"I'll be dog-damned!" Nort said. "It would even be easier, because they could use fax! It would record to disk from a fax program that didn't have any excess data! The fax has a message memory board that you can trace for awhile, but that would simply record from the same port! Damn!"

"Which means we won't get one byte of proof, because it doesn't exist, anymore," Bill pointed out. "I suppose you can get around that?"

"They don't use those old comps there, but there's a very important thing to note about them. The modem responds only to a specific directly dialed telephone number. The modem in those old things were nothing more than an answering machine is today."

"I'll be damned!" Bill exploded. "All we have to do is find the phone number they respond to and we can intercept, same as tapping a phone here.

"What that means ... Garner has an old Atari in his garage! He was a contact/relay point! He's not there most of the day, so we can get that thing and find the number to tap here!"

"Numbers. There will be two and they won't be in the comps, they'll be on disk somewhere."

"How do we find which disk?" Kersey asked.

"It will be an old low byte three point five floppy," Nort suggested. "We just check every ... *hah*!"

"Here, too!" Kersey said. "We'll have to find a way to get a warrant for that, though, and it will have to be for something else."

"Al, file that MP form for your wife! You can set up a surveillance camera or two in your house. Here's what we'll do.

"First, I'll call you and ask if you have...."

"Al? Nort here," greeted Al, when he got home from work that night. "I wanted to know if you have something. It's to do with this mess about Gorse and may be able to tie Levant to him, though we will probably still have to find the next link.

"When you filled out the form about your wife this morning you said you had some things at the office that could connect at least one of your neighbors to Levant? That would pretty automatically connect them right to Levant's killing."

"Well, I might have ... I'll have to run over to the office for part of it. I have the original things here. It's a few photos I took a couple of years ago ... yeah. I left the dates and locations on the list at the office. The pictures won't mean anything without the dates, and such and the dates and such are meaningless without the pictures.

"I'm having dinner with Alice and her husband tonight at that Italian restaurant by Corkscrew, so I can buzz over to the office and get the list from there and can bring the whole thing ... tell you what. Come over in the morning before eight and I'll give it to you and explain what it's all about, okay?"

"Sounds good to me! I'll see you in the morning!" Nort replied, and hung up.

Al worked for a few minutes setting up the three mini-videocams Bill gave him. They were tiny things that took startlingly clear pictures in poor light. He took some old photos showing a fishing trip with Landon when Gladys and Levant were both there, Levant in his boat and the rest of them in Landon's. He put the pictures in a manila envelope and put the phone book on it on the counter, then headed to the restaurant. Alice and Fred would be there. It was set up. The follower would see him go to the restaurant, then to the office, where he had a sheet with a bunch of dates and times plus a few locations typed out with a code by each entry.

He then went home about twelve thirty. The motion sensor operated videocams had been busy!

"Well, we have them both, plus the turkey you say was following you, on tape. They came by boat to your dock and in without anyone seeing them. They got the pictures," Bill said, smugly. "You will now get a phone call from your wife at work and she will give you a coded message of where to meet her. You will catch a flight to Mobile at 4:20. You will not go past the transfer at Atlanta, because they might have someone waiting in Mobile. You will stay among a lot of people until then, because they are going to be gunning for your ass. You might have another set of pictures or the negatives or something, and you still have the list. We can get and serve a warrant on them in about fifteen minutes.

"Let's go inside, where we can keep them occupied until an agent brings the warrant. I'm here, Nort is here, Kersey is here, and we'll have the squad who bring the warrant.

"George says he wants you as a special agent! You sure know how to place surveillance! He says there's not a blur or shadow to confuse anything!"

They went back inside, where Al kept complaining that the photos had been right there! On the counter! Under the phone book! Next to the phone! Somebody had been in his house, and he didn't feel secure at all, anymore!

When the cruiser and CSI team showed up with the warrant they demanded that Al go to work. He was perfectly willing to do that and to let them handle it!

He went.

The plane was being held on the runway at the last minute for a late-arriving passenger. It was an emergency.

Al thought about it and grinned to himself. He managed to be just inside the port when a man dodged in and said he was lucky he just made it aboard. He was explaining about some medical emergency. Al dodged out just as the port was closed and sealed. The flight attendant had stepped to show the passenger to his seat, so Al wasn't seen. He went down the tunnel, where a security guard saw him and yelled to stop. He said he had a panic attack and had to get off that plane. He had never flown before and didn't know what was happening. His heart was still going a mile a minute!

The guard said he'd seen a lot of that, but he should have had the attendant come off with him until they could explain. Al said the attendant was busy seating the last minute passenger, the door was still open, and he suddenly found himself running down the tunnel. He said he wouldn't hold it against the airline that his luggage was going to Mobile! He had paid for a ticket, so they owed him that and bringing it back!

The guard took his claim tickets and said he would arrange for the stuff to be returned, but Al would have to pay freight for that. It wasn't the airline's fault he was afraid of flying.

Finally he was able to get to a payphone to call Nort at home. He explained what had happened, and Nort promised he'd have the passenger checked on and detained, if his story didn't check out. Al had possibly saved his life, if he was a hit man.

Gloria Upton, who he knew, was on duty, so she'd come get him at the airport and take him to Nort's house. He could stay there with Trish until this mess was resolved, one way or another. They had found the comps and disks at Forbes' place and were going over them in the lab, but that would take time. They didn't have grounds to hold them without bail for breaking and entering, which was all they had. They didn't have the follower's ID, but there was no way they could hide him for long. The Forbes weren't going anywhere. There was a car waiting to follow them at ten feet if they tried to leave the house. If they took the boat, there wasn't anywhere they could go.

Al waited until Gloria showed up and went to Nort's. Trish and Jeanne cooked up a very good meal, they talked for awhile, then went to bed.

In the morning, the station called to say the Forbes were met at their dock by a boat and were gone. There didn't seem to be anyplace they could go, but they couldn't be found. They'd managed to give them the slip. Nort had it on speaker.

"Oh, crap!" Nort cried. "Why didn't you have someone watching from the dock side? We *knew* they could take a boat out of there!"

"We thought they'd take their own boat and Bill put a little tracer on it," Kersey explained. "We were going to let them lead us to whoever else is involved.

"We have what we need on the modem and old computer deal. It seems they have a set schedule of when they're getting a message and when they're sending one. It's in code, but it was easy to figure. They never thought anyone would ever see it. There's supposed to be a message in maybe an hour, so we'll see if it comes through. If not, they made a call from wherever they are not to use the connection.

"This is a mess! They're always one step ahead of us, and I still don't know what the *hell* it's about!"

"I have to call Bill!" Al exclaimed. "I think they're being very clever, but I think they've screwed up!

"Nort, this is a break! I think I know what it's about! I have to call Bill!"

"I can conference with him," Kersey said. "Give me a second to find which ... here it is."

There were about six rings, then Bill's sleepy voice, "Yeah? What?"

"Bill, Al here. Did you trace those phone numbers for the old comp setup?"

"It's at the lab, I suppose. What you got?"

"The Forbes have escaped. Another boat came and picked them up."

"*Shit*! They weren't expecting that?" he yelled.

"You told them to let them use their own boat, so they figured that's what they'd do. They're being clev...."

"Wait a damned minute!" Bill screeched. "*Where* are you? You're supposed to be in Atlanta by now!"

Al and Kersey quickly explained what had happened, and Kersey said the late passenger was being questioned about his ruse to get on that flight, but the turkey was claiming he just wanted to get to see his girlfriend because she was leaving him. No one swallowed that bit.

"So have them get in touch with the nonexistent girlfriend and his story is shot down."

"You're smart!" Bill agreed. "I think that's the first thing they'll think of. The noose, as the trite old saying goes, is tightening on that bunch."

"Well, that's all very neat," Kersey said, acidly. "Our part here is totally screwed! The Forbeses are gone! They've outsmarted us. Again! We'll get the evidence from the phone numbers they used with the old computer to tag them for Levant's murder, but we won't be able to tie them into Gorse's.

"Oh, well. One life without possibility of parole is as good as two. It just grinds that they might have outsmarted us again."

Al looked thoughtful, then grinned. "Not this time!"

"Well?" Bill asked, after a few seconds' silence.

"I think I know where you can find them, seeing the boat came for them," Al answered. "I don't know the address, but I know the name, and they're in Pelican's Perch. Paul Arnstein. They're friends, and they could get a boat in here and out up the creek without being seen until they were on their way into the place."

Nort grabbed a phone book and flipped through to say, "Paul S. Arnstein, Two two two two Haringtonian Circle" at about the same time Kersey said it.

"Hold on!" Bill said. "Get some cars in place, but I'll get a boat standing off their dock when you go in. They don't get to use the same trick twice!" They agreed and Al said he was sick of the crap and was going to work. Let him know how it comes out so he can get his wife home. He left. Trish said it was sort of fun, but also sort of scary.

Al came back in. "Hell! My car's at the airport!"

Nort laughed and Jeanne gave him the keys to her Honda. He gave his keys to Nort, and went out again. Nort would get his car and take it to his office, then would take Jeanne's back home to her after the raid on Arnstein's.

Al drove to his house to change clothes, then got his .32 automatic from the closet, checked it over and made sure the clip was full, then slipped it into his pocket. He found the old permit in the dresser drawer from when he used to carry the company funds to the bank every night, and headed for the office.

Nothing happened until a little after ten, when Nort called to say they had the whole bunch, except for the follower. He was going to have Trish stay at his place until they either found him or knew he was gone. They really wanted him, because he would complete their case for them. They could probably get a conviction without him, but definitely could with him.

Al went to lunch, then back to the office. He was watching all around as casually as he could. Nothing. He went home at the regular time and saw a certain car parked down the block on the side road before his place. He smirked to himself as he pulled into the drive, went to the mailbox, slipped the pistol into the mail when he got the keys to the house from his pocket, and went up the stairs to the front door and in. He went directly to the kitchen, where he stepped quickly to the side between the refrigerator and freezer. A dark figure came silently into the kitchen with a long fileting knife in his hand to stand looking around in confusion. He then moved silently toward the storeroom door and Al stepped out to put the .32 muzzle against his head just above the right ear.

"Gotcha!" Al hissed.

The man froze and dropped the knife. Al told him to sit in the chair at the table and punched Nort's number as he heard someone coming up the front steps. Nort answered and said to let Kersey and Bill in. They fully expected the follower to be there and wanted to be close enough to prevent anybody from being killed.

"What in the hell!?" Al cried. "He had a fileting knife! It would have taken him ten seconds to kill me!

"Come on in guys! It's open!"

"Nope! We knew you would be carrying the thirty two automatic registered to you and that you have an *expired* permit to carry!" Nort replied, laughing. "You have fifty times the smarts of that character! I could see by the look in your eyes when you left here that you had a plan.

"Trish says, can she come home now?"

"If there's not someone in this I don't know about, I was going to suggest it." Bill slapped the handcuffs on the follower. "I'll come after her in a little while. After I sign the statement or whatever."

"A little while? After you sign a statement? What, you don't know how a bureaucracy works?" Kersey said. "How about in about four hours, after signing a huge mountain of affidavits and forms?"

Al gave him the finger.

"Gotcha!" Bill said.

"Hon! Old Rocky's back!" Trish called from the deck as Al came from the kitchen with his coffee. "I guess you'll be drinking your coffee on the dock for awhile.

"Jeanne and Nort are coming over this afternoon, so Jeanne and I can go shopping while you and Nort can go fishing.

"Am I glad that stupid trial's over! I'll never understand why it took so long. They had them dead to rights!"

"It's the system. I suppose Bill finally found out what it's about. I don't accept the stupid story for one second, but it doesn't really matter, because that bunch is gone for good!"

"What story?"

"That they were only fighting a gang of terrorists who were plotting against Israel. They might have gotten someone to believe them if they'd said they were fighting terrorists who were plotting against this country, except that Gorse was no terrorist, Garner was no terrorist and Levant was no terrorist. At least, not against this country. They were all Jews and they're the terrorists in this case."

"Hon, is that a baby gator ... two of them ... climbing all over Old Rocky?" Trish asked.

Al studied them for a minute. There were two baby gators climbing all over Old Rocky.

"Well! It seems we were wrong about another thing!" Al said, laughing. "Now Old Rocky has to be renamed Old Rockette!"

C. D. Moulton's works are available on most major outlets as printed or e-books. CD writes the CD Grimes, PI, mysteries, the Det. Lt. Nick Storie mysteries, the Clint Faraday mysteries, the Flight of the Maita science fiction series, books on orchid culture and many others of many types. Mystery, adventure, intrigue, science fiction, humor, fantasy, paranormal, mild erotica, and factual.